F**K CUPCAKES AND F**K BAKING

M.E. CROFT

PORTICO

F**K OFF.

JUST KIDDING.

COME ON IN ...

Once upon a time, human beings existed solely on a diet of raw meat, fruit and vegetables. Those days are over. Now we are a nation of sweet tooths (or should that be teeth?), sugar fiends and muffin tops, hell bent on finding our next fix of freshly baked tastiness. Well, it has got to stop – before we reach bursting point.

*F**k Cupcakes and F**k Baking* is your alternative antidote to the current baking boom and global obsession with baked treats, bake offs, and cupcake boutiques, as well as the surprising uprising of baking programs on TV, not to mention the sickly-sweet websites and blogs that make you want to throw up all over your laptop.

This book will save your life*.

It will lower your cholesterol (as part of a healthy, balanced diet), as well as tickle your flabby funny bone and unsightly bingo wings. It's the perfect pocket-sized slice of pastry-related propaganda that will help you to rise up, take sweet revenge and say 'F**k you!' to cupcakes, baking and all the other cooking-related bollocks that is taking over our lives.

Now, put the baking tray down … back away from the oven … and go for a nice long walk, or something …

* Not legally binding.

THE RECAKEFICATION OF CUPS

Let's get one thing straight, before we go on any further, because there seems to be a lot of confusion out there in the ether.

Cupcakes are *not* a new invention. They haven't just appeared from nowhere as if by magic. Absolutely not.

These little harbingers of heart disease have actually been around since 1796. They were first mentioned in Amelia Simmons', *American Cookery*, the first-known cookbook to be written by an American. Now one cupcake is consumed for every adult in the USA every day. We've come a long way in going backwards, haven't we?

OK, now we can continue …

CAKESPIRACY THEORY #1

'Austerity, seriality, artistry, hybridity, that's what cupcakes are all about. The perfect food for our post-industrial, indie vibe Great Recession. Enjoy them while they last.'

Mark Sample, 'On the Predominance of Cupcakes as a Cultural Form'

CAKERCISE

Next time (i.e. in about a minute) you think about having a shop-bought cupcake that contains, on average, about 300–350 calories, just remember that it'll take you ages to burn off. Plus, you'll have to do exercise – and nobody wants to do that, do they? Especially if you are paying for gym membership.

The stats opposite *should* put you off wanting to eat cupcakes (or any baked treat, for that matter) for the rest of your life …

REMEMBER
ONE CUPCAKE = 350 CALORIES

ACTIVITY	CALORIES BURNED IN 30 MINS
Aerobics	149
Cycling	162
Dancing	130
Housework	117
Jogging	299
Shopping	78
Walking	104
Weight training	247

So, basically, you'd need to dance (vigorously, one assumes, not a slow dance) *for well over an hour* to burn off the required calories of just one lonely cupcake.

Still fancy that third cupcake?

FAIR TRADE?

While it is no secret that Americans are ridiculously huge food consumers (the largest on Earth by a country mile), what is not as well known is that they also throw away approximately half of the food they produce every year – worth around $165 billion.

In the USA the bread market is big business: the baking industry alone is worth over $30 billion dollars a year to the economy.

That said, figures from 2010 suggest that the average annual wage of a baker is $23,450 a year (or $11.27 an hour).

A loaf of bread, on average, in the USA costs $1.59.

NATIONAL CUPCAKE WEEK

In the UK National Cupcake Week 2013 kicks off on 16 September. Oh look, a gun …

'QU'ILS MANGENT DE LA BRIOCHE'

This famous French quote, translated in English as 'Let them eat cake' is usually attributed, incorrectly, to Queen Marie Antoinette after, it is said, she learnt of French peasants having no bread to eat. There is no record of her having ever said it, but it's a fun thing to say at birthday parties so that you sound smart.

Here is the phrase in other useful languages, so you can feel just as smug when you are abroad:

Que coman pasteles!
(Spanish)

Lad dem spise kage!
(Danish)

Far loro mangiare la torta
(Italian)

それらがケーキを食べてみましょう
(Japanese)

Et manducent crustulam!
(Latin)

Gadael iddynt fwyta cacen!
(Welsh)

Niech jedzą ciastka!
(Polish)

QUOTECAKES #1

'It must have been one of those Unidentified Flying Cupcakes ... a pigment of me imagination.'

Ringo Starr, *Yellow Submarine*

PRAIRIE OYSTER

Don't waste your last remaining eggs on baking stuff you don't really need to eat.

Use them to make a 'Prairie Oyster' – the world's most renowned, and beloved, hangover cure.

WHAT YOU'LL NEED

1 raw egg
1 teaspoon Worcestershire sauce
2 drops of Tabasco sauce
Salt and pepper

The protein in eggs help to rehydrate your cells. The copious amounts of alcohol you consumed last night will have dehydrated them to hell.

When you make this delectable concoction, try not to break the yolk, as the egg is supposed to give a similar sensation to eating an actual oyster. Half the fun of this cure is gagging on the yolk when you swallow it whole.

TEN BILLION BAGUETTES

The French population (around 65 million) eats approximately ten billion baguettes each year. That's half a baguette per person per day.

OTHER BAKING TRENDS TO IGNORE #1

It's not just cupcakes that have hit the baking big time, just you wait until these sticky treats get stuck into the mainstream …

CAKE POPS

Food blogger 'Bakerella' began the Cake Pop trend in 2008. Cake Pops are little balls of cake on a stick, dipped in anything you like – from chocolate and glitter to gold, frankincense and myrrh (probably) and decorated to look like anything from Humpty Dumptys to footballs. Around 170 calories per pop. And once you pop … you can't stop.

DONUT-ATHON

Over 10,000,000,000 donuts are made annually in the USA. That's a hole lot of donuts.

NOW WASH YOUR HANDS

In March 2013, Swedish furniture behemoth and divine meatball-makers Ikea, were forced to recall thousands of their almond cakes* (with chocolate and butterscotch) from its restaurants in 23 international stores after – wait for it – Chinese authorities found 'an excessive level' of coliform bacteria (or fecal matter) in two batches of cakes from a supplier in Sweden. Over 1,800 cakes had to be destroyed.

A vigil by cake fanatics across the world was held the next day in memory of the fallen delicacies. Some of the stores affected by the recall were located in Australia, China, France, Germany, Italy, Russia, Taiwan and the United Arab Emirates. Cakes in British and US stores were not affected or recalled. Those cakes were deemed poop-free.

* For legal reasons please note that the almond cakes are actually very delicious.

TOAST TO TOAST #1

According to Professor Tim Jacob at the School of Biosciences at Cardiff University in Wales, toast has *now been scientifically proven to be the UK's most loved feel-good food smell.*

While that sounds like the most ridiculous sentence ever (not to mention a waste of time, money and effort for the scientists who spent 20 years at school) the smell of toast, does apparently, trigger comforting and happy memories.

The report doesn't mention what feelings and memories are evoked by the smell of burnt toast though.

QUOTECAKES #2

Bart Simpson: 'It was an accident, ma'am!'
Judge Constance Harm: 'Don't spit on my cupcake and tell me it's frosting!'
Homer Simpson: 'What did she say about cupcakes?'

The Simpsons, 'The Parent Rap' (episode 271)

OUR DAILY BREAD* #1

There are tons of references to food in the Bible. Not many recipes though, which is a shame. It could use it.

Should you ever be stuck in a lift with a food-loving Christian, here are some handy quotes from the Bible to make small talk with. Don't laugh, it could happen …

And he took bread, and when he had given thanks, he broke it and gave it to them, saying, 'This is my body, which is given for you. Do this in remembrance of me.'
Luke 22:19

For the bread of God is he which cometh down from heaven, and giveth life unto the world.
John 6:33

So, whether you eat or drink, or whatever you do, do all to the glory of God.
Corinthians 10:31

It is good not to eat meat or drink wine or do anything that causes your brother to stumble.
Romans 14:21

* Matthew 6:11.

WEDDING CAKE

Cupcakes are now served at 13 per cent of weddings in the USA instead of the traditional wedding cake.

Divorce is up by 15 per cent – just saying.

MASTER BAKER

Dough-eyed bread hunk, Paul Hollywood, judge on the BBC's baking behemoth *The Great British Bake Off* and *The Great American Baking Competition* on CBS, is known in the baking world as a celebrity master baker.

His spiky silver hair, goatee and cuddly charms have made him a hit with the six million housewives in the UK who, along with watching the show, also tweet him some amazing puns …

@hollywoodbaker
You can squeeze my buns anytime

@hollywoodbaker
I knead you ;) XX

@hollywoodbaker
Pound cake me. No bun intended

@hollywoodbaker
Paul, you can put a bun in my oven

@hollywoodbaker
I thought I'd tweet you – muffin ventured muffin gained!

RECORD BAKERS #1

In January 1996, a bakery in Acapulco, Mexico went totally loco and baked the longest loaf ever produced.

The loaf was an astonishing 30,176ft (9,200m) long. Definitely a record to be scoffed (at).

CUPORIFIC

The Vanilla Cupcake, sold at the most well-known cupcake store* in the USA, contains a staggering 780 calories and 1⅕ oz (36g) of fat per cupcake – that's about half a woman's recommended daily allowance of fat.

* To remain anonymous, for fear of recrimination.

BAKING PUNS (TO NEVER DROP INTO CONVERSATION) #1

Next time you are having a pretentious conversation about baking with a self-proclaimed 'Foodie' (they're everywhere these days, so watch out), why not drop these terrible baking puns into conversation to annoy them. Hopefully then, they'll *leaven** you alone.

Bakers trade bread recipes on a knead to know basis.

A baker stopped making donuts after he got tired of the hole thing.

A good baker will rise to the occasion, it's the yeast he can do.

If you work in a bakery you may have to take on many rolls.

* *Leaven:* an agent, such as yeast, that causes dough to rise, especially by fermentation.

A BRIEF HISTORY OF THE SANDWICH

John Montagu, the 4th Earl of Sandwich (which is in Kent, England, if you didn't already know) was a notorious gambler. The invention of the sandwich came about, so the story goes, when the Earl asked his servant for 'a slice of meat between two slices of bread' so that the meal could be enjoyed without the Earl having to leave the gaming table.

In the UK, sandwiches now account for 50 per cent of the bread consumed.

THE WORLD'S MOST EXPENSIVE CUPCAKE

In July 2012 the cupcake community gasped collectively when the world's most expensive cupcake went on sale at Dubai's Bloomsbury Cupcakes store. Called the 'Golden Phoenix', it is – according to the people who sell them – no ordinary cupcake.

Made from the finest chocolate and parceled in edible sheets of 23-carat gold, as well as gold Ugandan vanilla beans and Premium Amedei Porcelena cocoa from Italy, without a doubt this cupcake represents a complete waste of creator, Shafeena Yusuff Ali's, time and energy.

Oh, and by the way, it cost Dh3,700 ($1,007/£645).

QUOTECAKES #3

'Who throws a cupcake? … Honestly!'

Young Dr Evil, *Goldmember*

BEST THING SINCE SLICED BREAD

The phrase 'The best thing since sliced bread' is bandied about as often as sliced bread itself. Ironically, the word 'bandied' is very rarely bandied about.

But do you actually know (or care?) when sliced bread was first sold? Well, I'll tell you …

In 1928, clever chappie Otto Frederick Rohwedder invented the first slice-and-wrap bread machine and sold sliced bread at his bakery in Battle Creek, Michigan, USA. It became very popular.

By 1933, 80 per cent of all bread sold in America came pre-sliced.

OTHER BAKING TRENDS TO IGNORE #2

MACAROONS

These meringue-based cookies filled with buttercream were invented in Italy in 1533. They became über popular in 2011, thanks to the US TV show *Gossip Girl*: they were Blair Waldorf's favorite things. There are around 140 calories per macaroon.

THE ELVIS

If you truly want to take your baking consumption to ridiculous levels, then f**k cupcakes entirely: they are puny weaklings in comparison to this calorific behemoth of a monster – the peanut butter, bacon and banana sandwich.

It is known as The Elvis, because it was the Warfarin-inducing weapon of choice for Elvis Presley – the King of rock and roll who died on his throne, stuffed to the gills with his beloved sandwiches and a whole host of other medicinal treats.

Fun to make, delicious to eat, but probably best shared with a few friends …

WHAT YOU'LL NEED

2 tablespoons butter, softened
8 slices white bread
½ cup/150g smooth peanut butter
1 large, ripe banana, sliced
¼ cup/100g honey
12 slices bacon, sautéed until crispy (optional)

LET'S GET IT ON!

Spread the butter on one side of each slice of bread. Spread peanut butter on the other side of half of the slices. Place banana slices on top of peanut butter. Drizzle honey over the bananas. Place three bacon slices on top of the banana, then place the remaining buttered bread slices on top, butter-side out.

Place sandwiches on a preheated grill pan or griddle. Flip them over when they become golden brown and crispy. When the sandwiches are browned on both sides, remove to plates. Slice in half and serve immediately.

PAIN IN THE ASS

Bread is so bad for you that even the French translation of the word itself is *pain*.

The average baguette contains ⅛ oz (3.75g) of fiber, and if eaten whole, would cause a massive pain in the ass.

CAKESPIRACY THEORY #2

'A cupcake is a model of modesty. And it's the best kind of modesty, because it paradoxically suggests extravagance. Cupcakes are rich. And expensive. You could buy two dozen Twinkies for the price of a single caramel apple spice gourmet cupcake.'

Mark Sample, 'On the Predominance of Cupcakes as a Cultural Form'

WORLD'S BIGGEST WASTE OF TIME

The world's biggest cupcake (so far, anyway) was built by the extreme cupcake fundamentalists Georgetown Cupcake in Sterling, Virginia. The cupcake weighs in at a belly bulging 2,594lb (1,177kg).

This silly record was officiated by the Guinness World Record monkeys on 2 November 2011. According to Guinness 'the cupcake was fully cooked and free standing with no support structures in place.' That's good to know, isn't it? The cupcake measured 56in (1.4m) in diameter, and 36in (91cm) tall and contained approximately 3 million calories.

BAKING THROUGH THE YEAR (abridged)

The USA – and some parts of the UK – take their 'food holidays' very seriously indeed. Here are some of the worst. (sorry, I mean best) that have been celebrated to date:

January 30 – National Croissant Day
International Pancake Day, every Shrove Tuesday
February 9 – National Bagel Day
National Hot Cross Bun Day, every Good Friday
March 4 – National Pound Cake Day
April 26 – National Pretzel Day
May 13 – National Apple Pie Day
May 19 – World Baking Day
June 1 – National Doughnut Day
July 30 – National Cheesecake Day
August 5 – National Waffle Day
September 27 – National Chocolate Milk Day
October 18 – National Chocolate Cupcake Day
November 21 – Gingerbread Day
December 15 – National Cupcake Day

Hilariously, 21 July is National Junk Food Day. Surely that's not something to celebrate.

BEYOND AWFUL BAKING JOKES #1

What's the fastest cake in the world?

... *scone.*

BROWNIES

BROWNIES *NOUN*

Small, delicious squares of moist, baked chocolatey deliciousness. Should contain nuts.

BROWNIES *HUMAN*

Members of a British Girl Guides organization for girls aged 7–10 years old. Should *not* contain nuts.

QUOTECAKES #4

'Mini cupcakes?
As in the mini version of regular cupcakes?
Which is already a mini version of cake?
Honestly, where does it end with you people?'

Kevin Malone, *The Office US*

EMBARRASSING DESSERTS

Admit it, baking is embarrassing. You wouldn't be seen dead ordering these desserts in a fancy restaurant and if you do, titters always ensue.

1. **Spotted Dick** – a steamed suet pudding.
2. **Sticky Buns** – a roll of leavened dough, sweetened with sugar or cinnamon.
3. **Blow Pops** – a lollipop with a bubble gum center, then encased in a hard shell.
4. **Buttered Crumpet** – a crumpet with butter on.
5. **Banana Split** – an ice cream dessert served with whipped cream, cherries, sweet topping and a banana 'split' in two.
6. **Iced Fingers** – a moist rectangular pastry with an iced sugar topping.
7. **Dean's Cream** – a trifle-esque sweet dessert.
8. **Eton Mess** – strawberries and cream, on a meringue base.
9. **Wet Nelly** – a hard-bread pudding.
10. **Syllabub** – a rich, creamy, lightly curdled pudding seasoned with sugar and wine.

BREAKING BREAD #1

While 99 per cent of households in the UK buy bread, a recent report said that 44 per cent of men eat bread twice a day (presumably breakfast toast and sandwich lunch), compared to just 25 per cent of women (who are trying to cut down on the carbs).

RECORD BAKERS #2

If the reason you are reading this book is because you know you have become addicted to baking, and this is part of your 12 Step Program to admitting you have a problem, then a) thanks for buying the book, b) congratulations and c) take comfort in the fact that a bunch of even bigger losers spent a large portion of their lives making the world's largest chocolate chip cookie, as officiated by the *Guinness Book of World Records*, on 17 May 2003:

Made by the Immaculate Baking Company in Flat Rock, North Carolina the cookie measured 8,120 sq. ft (754 sq. m), weighed 40,000lb (18 tonnes) and had a diameter of 101ft (30m).

To give a sense of scale, a Blue Whale – the largest mammal on Earth – is approximately the same size.

DONUT DAY

The first National Donut Day, yes there is such a thing, was held in 1938 as a fundraiser for the Salvation Army in Chicago.

THE GREAT BRITISH RUB OFF

Thanks to the phenomenal ongoing success of the BBC's *Great British Bake Off*, food analysts from all over the country can now proudly report utter meaningless statistics such as the fact that 7.2 million people watched the series finale on 16 October 2012. This figure represented 25 per cent of the overall viewing audience for its timeslot – pre-watershed, obviously. And there's this one.

The Top Five items baked in the UK in 2012:

1. **Standard cake** (e.g. Victoria Sponge, Carrot Cake etc.)
2. **Small cakes** (e.g. Cupcakes)
3. **Batters** (e.g. Pancake, Yorkshire Pudding)
4. **Biscuits/cookies**
5. **Sweet puddings** (e.g. Crumble, Pavlova)

BEST MAN SPEECH OPENING LINE

If you're a baking fanatic and due to be the Best Man at a wedding, you could do worse than opening your speech with this line …

'It's been an emotional day … even the cake is in tiers.'

TOAST TO TOAST #2

The wonderful people at the British Flour Advisory Bureau (whose aim is to promote the role of flour and bread as part of a balanced diet through educational material, apparently) discovered in a recent survey that the UK is a nation of toast lovers with over 99 per cent of people claiming they 'simply love toast'. Their words not mine.

42 per cent of the two million students heading off to university in the UK said that 'Toast would remind them of home and hence evoke feelings of comfort'.*

* 100 per cent of the students were drunk when the survey was conducted.

OTHER RIDICULOUS FOOD FADS HEADING YOUR WAY

The last three years have given rise to many ridiculous baking trends. From celebrity chefs to organic produce, multiple bake off TV shows to cupcake boutiques, blogs and websites.

To give the world's current love of cupcakes some much-needed context, here is a list of other five baking trends that are currently making everybody's skin itch with excitement in 2013:

1. **Peek-a-boo cakes** – cakes with decorated insides, so when you slice them open your eyes get a treat too.
2. **Marshmallows** – unique high-end flavors like licorice and beetroot are most popular. Flumps are dead, it seems.
3. **Zebra cakes** – cakes with a stripy sponge, you know, like a zebra.
4. **Éclairs** – big in Paris right now – so the tastemakers claim.
5. **Donuts** – but not just a regular donut. God no. These are artisan donuts with unique flavor combinations like bubble and squeak. They sound awful.

THE WINNER BAKES IT ALL

The UK baking industry is worth £3.4 billion a year.

While that is nowhere near as big as the value of the US baking industry, what is astonishing is that, on average *12 million loaves of bread are sold every single day in the UK.*

QUOTECAKES #5

'Well, that's real swell, but it still doesn't get the cream in the cupcake.'

Samantha Jones, *Sex and the City*

BEAT IT, SUGAR #1

When it comes to baking, sugar is in everything. Even bread. Lots of it.

I don't want to give you nightmares, but here's some really scary sugar facts that – along with all the sugar you are eating – will keep you up at night:

* By weight, sugar accounts for approximately 9 per cent of all food eaten in the USA.

* The average American consumes a coma-welcoming 2–3lb (1–1.4kg) of sugar every week.

* In the American diet alone, sugar accounts for 496 calories a day. That's a quarter of your recommended daily intake.

* Forty times more sugar is consumed now per person in the USA than in 1750.

BREAKING BREAD #2

White bread accounts for 76 per cent of the bread sold in the UK.

Wholemeal bread is acknowledged, on the whole, to be healthier for you.

The UK is 100 per cent a nation of idiots.

CAKE ON THE WEB

Google is a pretty good indicator of popularity these days. Judging by these results, it seems our baked treats have lots of friends*.

Cake – 542,000,000 results
Cupcake – 109,000,000 results
Chocolate cake – 109,000,000 results
Baking – 170,000,000 results
Brownie – 43,100,000 results
Muffin – 60,500,000 results
and
How fat am I? – 748,000,000 results

* Correct at time of printing. Figures have probably quadrupled by now.

NOT SO FAIRY CAKE

Just as Britain's fairy cakes are regarded as a poor person's American-style cupcakes, these days donuts are often considered the *very* poor person's cupcake – their popularity has diminished since their glory days in the 1990s, when they were the go-to treat in the USA. But don't kid yourself, donuts have still got it going on, in the wallet department …

In the USA the donut industry is worth $3.6 billion a year.

MARY, MARY QUITE CONTRARY #1

'Even if money is short, it doesn't cost much to bake a scone. If you're feeling a little bit down, a little bit of kneading really helps.'

Mary Berry, baking expert, food writer, presenter of BBC TV's *The Great British Bake Off* and all round living 'legend'

NOW YOU KNOW #1

A *single whole grain* of wheat makes over 20,000 particles of flour.

However, it takes around *350 ears* of wheat to make just enough flour for one standard loaf of bread.

Remember that the next time you throw away a few slices of bread, simply because you 'think they look bad'.

SEX AND THE CITY #1

The cupcake boom in the USA (and therefore globally) can largely be attributed, rather ridiculously, to an episode of TV show *Sex and the City*. The episode entitled 'No Ifs, Ands or Butts' showed Carrie Bradshaw munching happily on a Magnolia Bakery cupcake. The episode first aired on 9 June 2000.

DONUT FORGET ME

Donuts (or ye olde doughnuts, depending on which side of the pond you are on) were – it is agreed – first brought to North America by Dutch settlers in the 18th century in the form of 'olykoek', a fried doughball that literally translates as 'oil cake'. Surely that should have rung alarm bells …

CAKEPRENEURS

The Great British Bake Off has not only led to a 95 per cent rise in apron sales (probably), there has also been a massive rise in baking business start-ups, referred to as 'cakepreneurs' (not by me), since 2010. Here are some percentages for you, which, horrifyingly, are all true.

* 325 per cent increase in cake making businesses since 2009.
* 54 per cent increase in start-up cake making businesses.
* Cake baking rises to eighteenth most popular start-up business idea in Britain.
* 91 per cent of the 'cakepreneurs' are women, though there has been a slight increase in male bakers, from 8 per cent in 2010 to 9 per cent in 2011.
* The majority of cake businesses are being started by people in their 20s and 30s.

GET STUFFED

The record for consuming 49 glazed donuts in eight minutes is held by fruitcake Eric Booker. It was officiated by the International Federation of Competitive Eating (IFOCE) so it's a genuine 'record'. I'm sure Eric's mum was very proud.

TERMS OF ENCAKEMENT

There are lots of baking-related terms of endearment currently doing the rounds in popular vernacular. You've probably been called one – or more – if you're unlucky.

Here are ten of the worst.

1. Cupcake
2. Muffin
3. Sweetie pie
4. Puddin' pop
5. Pumpkin
6. Jellybean
7. Quiche Lorraine (if you're called Lorraine)
8. Frangipani (if you're feeling exotic)
9. Tart (if you're feeling rude)
10. Sugar tits (if you're Mel Gibson)

RIDICULOUS BAKING SHOWS TO AVOID

Bakers in the USA have moved to a whole new level of OTT baking, thanks to the Food Network – a 24-hour channel devoted to sticking sickly-sweet things into ovens. The five most outrageously addictive shows are:

1. 'Cupcake Wars'

'Each week on "Cupcake Wars", four of the country's top cupcake bakers face off in three elimination challenges until only one decorator remains. The sweet prize: $10,000.'

2. 'Ace of Cakes'

'Meet Chef Duff. Shaping cakes with drill saws and blowtorches, and staffing his bakery with fellow rock musicians, he's not your typical baker. However, he's one of the most sought-after decorative cake makers in the country. Every week at Charm City Cakes in Baltimore, Duff and his team of artists try to meet the demands of creating up to 20 cakes a week, some of which take up to 29 hours to build!'

3. 'Glutton For Punishment'

'Bob Blumer loves a challenge. One week he's training for the National Oyster Shucking Contest, the next he's juggling razor-sharp knives in a crash course to become a Benihana chef. Fun, fast-paced and entertaining, this is a show for passionate foodies and armchair adventurers.'

4. 'Have Cake, Will Travel'

This show '… follows Ashley Vicos, the reigning queen of the cake decorating world, and her team around the country as they create extraordinary, one-of-a-kind cakes for special events from New York's Fashion Week to Mardi Gras in New Orleans.'

5. 'Sugar High'

'Duff Goldman takes a cross-country trek to capture the sweet secrets and tasty techniques that keep the cookies from crumbling in the top bakeries around the nation.'

HALF-BAKED ON WASTED TREATS

Human beings are a race of wasters, you don't need me to tell you that. But what you do need me to tell you is that *2.6 billion slices of bread* – that's 32 per cent of all bread purchased by UK households – are thrown away each year in the UK, wasted, when they could have been eaten by yours truly.

775 million bread rolls a year are thrown out on their ear too – and they did nothing wrong either.

It is also estimated that *1.2 million pastries* are put out to pasture simply because they were unloved before their sell-by date.

QUOTECAKES #6

'You never know what you're writing when you write a song, it's only years later you realize the truth. You think you're writing about other people, but you're really just writing about cupcakes.'

John Lennon, British singer-songwriter

FACEBAKE*

2,137,271 people have gone out of their way to 'like' baking on Facebook.

1,246,108 people have gone out of their way to 'like' cupcakes on Facebook.

283,804 people have gone out of their way to 'like' chocolate brownies on Facebook.

99,169 people have gone out of their way to 'like' muffins on Facebook.

* Figures correct at time of printing.

OTHER BAKING TRENDS TO IGNORE #3

FROZEN YOGHURT

Frozen yoghurt is yoghurt that is, er, frozen, and contains around 200 calories for the full fat variety. Look, if you're going to have dessert, just have ice cream, OK?

PUPCAKES *NOUN*

I suppose it was inevitable. The very minute the cupcake craze started, it was only a matter of time before the trend trickled downward to our poor, stupid (but loyal) canine friends.

Pupcakes, or cupcakes for dogs, are another food fad that threatens to go mainstream in 2014. With recipes to cure your dog of bad breath or simply beef up their diet, pupcakes come in a staggering variety of choices and have been labeled 'a healthy gourmet treat for dogs'.

Interestingly, approximately 35 per cent of all dogs in Britain are overweight.

MARY, MARY QUITE CONTRARY #2

'It's a bit of joy in the middle of this recession. You watch a programme like this and begin to feel warm again. It's what life is all about.'

Mary Berry, baking expert, food writer, presenter of BBC TV's *The Great British Bake Off* and all round living 'legend'

OUR DAILY BREAD #2

More food-related Bible quotes to live your life by …

For life is more than food, and the body more than clothing.
Luke 12:23

Or do you not know that your body is a temple of the Holy Spirit within you, whom you have from God? You are not your own.
Corinthians 6:19

For anyone who eats and drinks without discerning the body eats and drinks judgment on himself.
Corinthians 11:29

It is not what goes into the mouth that defiles a person, but what comes out of the mouth; this defiles a person.
Matthew 15:11

He shall eat curds and honey when he knows how to refuse the evil and choose the good.
Isaiah 7:15

CUPCAKE ATM

In 2012 Sprinkles Cupcakes in Beverly Hills, California, opened their first cupcake ATM. It is exactly what you think it is.

A 'first-of-a-kind', this machine acts like an ordinary hole-in-the-wall: you put in your credit card, order your cupcakes via an electronic touch-screen and – bingo – seconds later your order arrives through a slot. It has to be seen to be believed … but it exists, I assure you. Only in Hollywood …

BEYOND AWFUL BAKING JOKES #2

Why not try out this classic baking joke for size* next time you leave the house.

What do you call someone with jelly in
one ear and custard in the other?
A trifle deaf.

* Probably large.

PASTRY SAINT

Saint Honoré, of Amiens, France (*d.*600 AD), is the patron saint of Pastry chefs and bakers.

I know, I know – the fact that there is even a Baking Saint makes the process of canonization look even sillier than it is anyway.

What next? Saint Prius the Patron Saint of hybrid automobiles?

SEX AND THE CITY #2

According to the *New York Post*, the flagship store of the Magnolia Bakery in the West Village, which famously provided the cupcakes for the episode of *Sex and the City*, and thus single-handedly kick-started the worldwide love affair with cupcakes, was shut down in February 2013.

The West Village cupcake store was inspected by the New York City Department of Health and Mental Hygiene and five 'critical violations' were reported. The department claimed it found mouse holes and mouse feces, as well as evidence of live rats, mice and flies, but it has since reopened. Carrie Bradshaw would not be impressed.

PIE-THYGORAS

As unbelievable, and unhealthy, as it may sound, sales of pork pies alone make up £145 million of a supermassive £1 billion pie industry in the UK.

CAKESPIRACY THEORY #3

'By the very nature of their production, cupcakes are made in multiples. A 3 x 3 tray of nine cupcakes or 4 x 4 tray of 16 cupcakes, it doesn't matter. Cupcakes are serial cakes: mass produced, but conveying a sense of home-style goodness.

Cupcakes are the perfect homeopathic antidote for the industrially produced food we mostly consume. Fordism never tasted so sickly sweet.'

Mark Sample, 'On the Predominance of Cupcakes as a Cultural Form'

COOKIES

COOKIE *NOUN*

Small, flat baked treat made up of flour, eggs, sugar and usually containing chunks of chocolate. Can cause excessive weight gain.

COOKIE *HTTP*

A cookie, also referred to as an HTTP cookie or web cookie, is a piece of data sent from an Internet website (and then stored in a web browser) while a person is browsing a website for three hours straight. Can also cause excessive weight gain.

BAKED FOR SUCCESS

Recent surveys report that the UK's current baking boom is set to stick around for a long time. It also throws up some interesting statistics.

If you want to blame anyone, and you should, then blame the baking shows … and throw some of these horrifying stats at the presenters if they are ever brave enough to step out onto the streets …

* 41 million Brits (roughly 79 per cent of adults) bake at home.
* Seven out of ten (68 per cent) men bake at home in the UK (though presumably not those who support Manchester United).
* 23 per cent of adults bake at least once a week.
* 3 million people in the UK bake every day.
* 22 per cent (roughly nine million) of home bakers claim to have upped their baking since the airing of the first series of the BBC's *Great British Bake Off.* The market for home baking rose a whopping 59 per cent between 2007 and 2012 and is now worth £1.7 billion.

BEYOND AWFUL BAKING JOKES #3

How do you make an apple turnover?

Push it down a hill.

BAKING BOOM

In the USA, the 'cupcake industry', as I am loathed to call it, is a $250 million industry with three years of solid growth since 2010.

USE YOUR LOAF

The language of England's wide boys and hard men, Cockney rhyming slang, is actually pretty synonymous with the girly underworld of baking.

Here are some truly heinous bits of slang you should think carefully about using before you open your 'north and south'.

Apples and pears – stairs
Bacon and eggs – legs
Biscuits and cheese – knees
Butcher's hook – look
Loaf of bread – head
Mince pies – eyes
Rabbit and pork – talk
Raspberry tart – fart
Brown bread – dead
Jam jar – car
Plates of meat – feet
Porky pies – lies
Raspberry ripple – nipple
Ruby Murray – curry
Syrup of figs – wig

WISDOM OF CROWDS (I.E. TWITTER) #1

'Cupcakes are just muffins who went to fashion school.' #Cupcakes #quote #fashion

rolls eyes

SYMPTOMS OF DIABETES

A lot of you are eating more cupcakes and sweetened baked goods than you used to, so just so we are all clear, you know, in case of an emergency:

ARE YOU?

* Feeling very thirsty?
* Urinating frequently, particularly at night?
* Feeling very tired?
* Noticing weight loss and loss of muscle bulk (in type 1 diabetes)?

SPRINKLES EARNS HUNDREDS OF THOUSANDS

Sprinkles Cupcakes, in Beverly Hills, California, is commonly regarded as the first cupcake-only bakery in the world. The business was founded by two former investment bankers, Candace Nelson and her husband, at a time when the baking industry was actually experiencing a four-year decline. Not put off by this, they chased their dream, and only three hours into their first day of business all their cupcakes had sold out.

At the end of their first week they had sold 2,200 cupcakes; the craze had begin. Life for all of us has never been the same again.

QUOTECAKES #7

'I've never met a problem a proper cupcake couldn't fix.'

Sarah Ockler, American author

GDAs

In 1998, some bright sparks in the British Government (there are some apparently), the food industry and 'consumer organizations' (whoever they are) came up with Guideline Daily Amounts or GDAs.

This acronym (which sounds a lot like an Australian saying 'Hello') is actually a pretty miserable way of looking at how we consume food. GDAs detail, rather strictly, how much energy and key nutrients the 'average person' (whoever they are) is allowed per day – according to the Government, the food industry and 'consumer organizations' (whoever they are). The point being, I guess, that if you consume more than your GDA, you get fat and die.

Here's a cheerful reminder of what the Government says you are allowed to eat.

	Men	Women
Fat (total)	3⅕ oz (96g)	3⅕ oz (96g)
of which saturates	1oz (30g)	⅔ oz (20g)
Salt	⅕ oz (6g)	⅕ oz (6g)
Sugar*	4oz (120g)	3oz (90g)

* Total sugars include sugars that naturally occur in foods.

TAKE A STAND

Sales of traditional cake stands in the UK are up an unbelievable 207 per cent since 2012 – the biggest rise among all types of baking equipment.

ONE BILLION EGGS

One cupcake is consumed for every adult in the USA every day – that's 250 million cupcakes. Using the famous 1-2-3-4 cupcake recipe (the name derives from the fact that it uses 1 cup of butter, 2 cups of sugar, 3 cups of flour and 4 eggs) that works out as 250 million cups of butter, 500 million cups of sugar, 750 million cups of flour … and 1 BILLION eggs consumed every day. And that's just for cupcakes.

WISDOM OF CROWDS (I.E. TWITTER) #2

'Love is like a good cupcake. You never know when it's coming, but you better eat it when it does.'
@CupcakesQuotes

rolls eyes again

LARGE HOLE

The inexplicably sexy-sounding Randy's Donuts in Inglewood, California, has the largest donut statue in the whole of the USA, measuring 22ft (6.7m) in diameter. You read that right, *statue* ... praise be!

CAKE ON TV

Watching an hour's worth of baking shows can add an extra 250 calories to an adult's daily intake, researchers have suggested recently.

There are (I've counted) 25 different baking shows on UK TV channels each and every evening (excluding the actual Food Network). If you watched every single one of these shows you'd potentially double your recommended 2,500 calories allowed per day.

So maybe turn over and watch the news, instead? The grim horrors of reality are much more slimming.

BAKING PUNS (TO NEVER DROP INTO CONVERSATION) #2

Baking puns are not big and they're not clever. Anyone caught using a baking pun is a self-raising moron.

Working in the bakery left her with a loathe of bread.

The local baker was paying his staff based on a flourly rate.

The father who worked as a baker was a real breadwinner.

After burning a batch of cookies a baker felt very crummy.

COOKING THE BOOKS #1

£126,400,000*

The total value of cookery book sales of food wünderkind, global icon and Naked Chef himself, Jamie Oliver

* That's approximately 10 million books sold.

DEATH BY PUDDING

Here are ten of the worst types of pudding you can eat. Not in terms of their taste, but in terms of their ability to clog your arteries and stop your heart from beating.

So, if you want to spend the afternoon baking, that's fine, just don't come knocking on my door when you get profiteroles stuck on your lungs.

(Check back to GDAs on page 84 for your daily allowance.)

	AV. PORTION	CALORIES	FAT
Bakewell tart	4oz (120g) slice	547	¾ oz (22.5g)
Cheesecake	3⅓ oz (100g) slice	426	1¼ oz (37.5g)
Treacle tart	3oz (90g)	341	⅖ oz (12g)
Chocolate cake	3⅔ oz (110g) slice	340	⅖ oz (12g)
Apple pie	3⅔ oz (110g) slice	293	½ oz (15g)
Trifle	5oz (150g)	249	⅖ oz (12g)
Chocolate éclairs	2¼ oz (67.5g)	244	⅗ oz (18g)
Pavlova	2¾ oz (82.5g)	230	⅓ oz (10g)
Pancakes	2oz (60g)	181	⅓ oz (10g)
Chocolate mousse	2oz (60g)	89	⅛ oz (3.75g)

THE GREAT FIRE OF LONDON

In September 1666 London was gutted – both literally and emotionally – by a massive fire that destroyed most of the city. The fire started, of course, in a stupid bakery.

So, next time you're in London and visit a bakery, recite these following facts at the baker and ask for a serious discount on your next purchase.

* In 1559, a writer called Daniel Baker predicted that a big fire would devastate London. No one listened to him – presumably because he was a baker.
* Like the weather leading up to the Great Chicago Fire of 1871, the summer of 1666 had been long and dry. Much of the city's water supplies had been used up during droughts caused by the hot weather.
* The fire started at about 2 o'clock in the morning on Sunday 2 September 1666, at Thomas Farynor's bakers in Pudding Lane. One of the workers smelled smoke and woke his boss and his family. The family fled across the street, but one of the household's maids refused to leave. She became one of the first people to be killed by the fire.

* 370 acres of the city were destroyed.
* 13,000 houses were burnt down. They were made of wood, to be fair.
* Officially only four people died, but the actual number is probably a lot higher.
* 84 churches were not saved.
* 100,000 people were made homeless.
* In today's money, the cost of the fire would have been £1 billion.
* Samuel Pepys, the great English diarist, was forced to leave his home during the fire, but not before he had buried some prized possessions including wine and Parmesan cheese – but no bread.

So, bakers were to blame for the largest fire in London's history (unlike in Chicago where a cow was to blame) – as well as your burgeoning waistline. Bunch of troublemakers, aren't they?

CELEBRITY CUPCAKES

Herewith lie the Top Ten famous* celebrity 'cupcakes' – according to the online blogs and tweets of 'tweenagers' who found them 'utterly delicious'.

Also, here are ten reasons to hate 'cupcake' as a term of male appreciation.

1. Harry Styles
2. Justin Bieber
3. The Jonas Brothers
4. Cody Simpson
5. Greyson Chance
6. Taylor Lautner
7. Robert Pattinson
8. Josh Hutcherson
9. Zac Efron
10. Freddie Highmore

* You're doing very well if you don't know who any of these people are.

BLAME CHURCHILL

Winston Churchill was, supposedly, the first person in the history of the whole world (and remember, cupcakes had been around since 1796) to suggest a sweet frosting be splurged on top of the cakes. So, if you want anyone to blame for your waistline, blame Churchill. He later blamed the frosting for his enormous jowls. No argument there, Winston.

AWFUL MUFFIN JOKE

Two muffins were baking in an oven.
One muffin looked at the other and said, 'Hey man, is it getting hot in here?'
The other muffin said, 'Arghh! You can talk!'

THE WI

Baking is so hot right now that it has been reported that Britain's Women's Institutes (community-based organizations for women, founded in 1915) has had 56,500 new young women sign up to branches across England and Wales since 2009. Their total membership now stands at 210,000.

DONUT BOTHER

A glazed donut contains a sweat-inducing 200 calories. You'd have to go for a very long walk in blazing heat for a couple of hours to work that off. Is it worth it?

MUFFIN TOP

The world has become so obsessed with baking (and the eating of baked goods) that we have created a baking-related term to describe what happens when you eat too many things that are baked. Mad, isn't it?

Ladies and gentleman, I give you …

MUFFIN TOP *NOUN, INSULT*

A derogatory term that describes the overhanging body fat that visibly spills over the waistline of a female's skirt or trouser. The look resembles a muffin spilling out over its paper casing.

Muffin top was added to the *Oxford English Dictionary** in 2011.

* Online edition.

DEATH BY PASTRY

God works in mysterious ways. And pastry is one of them. Why is something so undeniably bad for you, just so bloody delicious? Not fair.

(Check back to GDAs on page 84 for your daily allowance.)

	AV. PORTION	CALORIES	FAT	SAT. FAT
Beef pie	5oz (150g)	449	1oz (30g)	⅖ oz (12g)
Cornish pasty	5oz (150g)	414	⅞ oz (25g)	⅓ oz (10g)
Pork pie	1⅔ oz (50g)	196	⅖ oz (12g)	⅕ oz (6g)
Sausage rolls	2oz (60g)	230	⅗ oz (18g)	¼ oz (7.5g)
Quiche Lorraine	3⅓ oz (100g)	175	¼ oz (7.5g)	⅕ oz (6g)

As delicious as Cornish pasties may be, are they really worth the trip to the Emergency Room?

UPCAKES

According to a recent report, between 2010 and 2011 there was a 52 per cent increase in cupcake consumption in the UK.

QUOTECAKES #8

‘God gives us the ingredients for “Our Daily Bread”, but he expects us to do the baking.’

Unknown

ROLL WITH IT

Greggs, the popular British high street baker, sells more than 140 million sausage rolls a year. That's 2.7 million a week; or nearly 400,000 a day.

FAT JOKES

Nobody wants to be the butt of fat jokes, especially if you have Big Bone condition, which close friends tell me is not nice at all. But kids can be cruel and, let's be honest, fat jokes are hilarious – even fat people agree, so that makes it OK.

The truth is, if you eat a lot of cake, the chances are you would have heard some terribly demeaning fat jokes that probably would have made you laugh out loud, if only you didn't have cake in your mouth at the time.

Here are four of my favorite fat jokes that will definitely have you wobbling with mirth.

Your mum is so fat I took a picture of her last Christmas … and it's still printing.

Your mum is so fat that if she jumped in the air, she'd get stuck.

Your mum is so fat, she had her baby pictures taken by satellite.

BAKECENTAGES

Ridiculous as this sounds, since series two of the BBC's *The Great British Bake Off* aired in 2010, sales of baking trays in the UK have increased by 25 per cent.

REAL MEN DON'T EAT QUICHE

Most men can see clearly now Lorraine has gone, but as American author Bruce Feirstein once famously wrote in his bestselling novel, *Real Men Don't Eat Quiche*, er, 'real men don't eat quiche'.

Feirstein's book is, according to Wikipedia (I've not actually read it), 'a tongue-in-cheek book satirizing stereotypes of masculinity'.

This masterpiece 'popularized the term "quiche eater", in an attempt to refer to a man who is a dilettante, a trend chaser, an over-anxious conformist to fashionable forms of "lifestyle" and socially correct behaviors and opinions, one who eschews the traditional masculine virtue of tough-self assurance'. Sounds terrible.

In honor of this piece of work, I've consulted the Internet and compiled a list of ten other things real men apparently don't do.

1. Real men don't wear pyjamas.
2. Real men don't iron their shirts.
3. Real men don't need recipes.
4. Real men don't pay overdue bills.
5. Real men don't play with kittens.
6. Real men don't put the toilet seat down.
7. Real men don't read instruction manuals.
8. Real men don't 'like' things on Facebook.
9. Real men don't pay attention when driving a car.
10. Real men don't go to hospital after falling off a roof.

QUOTECAKES #9

'You've baked a really lovely cake, but then you've used dog shit for frosting.'*

Steve Jobs, co-founder of Apple Inc., commenting on a NeXT programmer's work

* iPoo, anyone?

A CAKE BY ANY OTHER NAME

Thinking of starting a cupcake business? Of course you are. Who isn't?

Naming a cupcake business is probably the best part of owning a cupcake business. Though surely the novelty wears off after the 3,000th time you say 'Welcome to Kickass Cupcakes', but that's the cost of doing business.

Here are some of the 'best' names of cupcake shops from around the world.

1. Kickass Cupcakes
2. BabyCakes
3. Crumbs Bakery Shop
4. Crème De La Cupcake
5. Cup of Cake
6. Cupcakery
7. Cupcake Crazy
8. Get Baked Cupcakes
9. Le Cupcake
10. Makey Bakey Cakey
11. Pompous Cupcakes

COOKING THE BOOKS #2

Sales of cookery books in the UK increased by a mega 250 per cent in 2012.

Are people any better at baking because of this? Computer says no.

BAKING ABBREVIATIONS

Text-speak, like baking, has infiltrated every nook and cranny of modern culture. And while there are traditional baking abbreviations (tsp, tbsp, oz, ml, kg, etc.) there are also a few more quirky baking abbreviations …

LOL	Left Over Loaf
ROFL	Really Old Focaccia Left
WTF	Where's The Flour?
BTW	Bread That's Wilted
OMG!	Oh Melt, God-damn-you!
IMHO	Incinerated My Hot Oats
MILF	Meringue Is Looking Funny
KWIM	Kitchen Will Inevitably (be) Messy
KC	Knead Chocolate
PITA	Pudding Is Too Alcoholic
YOLO	Yeast Only Leavens Once

OUR DAILY BREAD #3

And here's another helping of food-based Bible quotes …

By the sweat of your face you shall eat bread, till you return to the ground, for out of it you were taken; for you are dust, and to dust you shall return.
Genesis 3:19

Did you not pour me out like milk and curdle me like cheese?
Job 10:10

And they gave him a piece of a cake of figs and two clusters of raisins. And when he had eaten, his spirit revived, for he had not eaten bread or drunk water for three days and three nights.
1 Samuel 30:12

He will take your daughters to be perfumers and cooks and bakers.
1 Samuel 8:13

CAKESPIRACY THEORY #4

'A cupcake's not really a cake. A distant cousin to the muffin, maybe. Is it a pastry for the 21st century United States, a kind of American croissant, full of gooey American exceptionalism? The cupcake itself doesn't even know what it is. It's a hybrid form, a Frankencaken.'

Mark Sample, 'On the Predominance of Cupcakes as a Cultural Form'

MANCAKES

Cupcakes are no longer the preserve of young girls and housewives. Nope, in these modern days of metro sexuality, men are climbing aboard the cupcake craze and getting their hands dirty (with cake mixture).

The Internet has spawned a million manly baking websites, most famously, www.butchbakery.com that features its own MAN-ifesto. 'Butch it up, these ain't your grandma's cupcakes, buttercup. Our objective is simple. We're men. Men who like cupcakes. Not the frilly pink-frosted sprinkles-and-unicorns kind of cupcakes. We make manly cupcakes. For manly men.'

Examples of the manly kind of cupcakes you can order are:

The B-52 – 'A Kahlua-soaked Madagascar cake with Bailey's Bavarian filling.'
Sidecar – 'A brandy-soaked cake with orange brandy buttercream.'
Driller – 'A maple cake topped with crumbled bacon loaded with milk chocolate buttercream.'

Basically, they all have booze or meat in them.

QUOTECAKES #10

'Nothing seems to please a fly so much as to be taken for a currant; and if it can be baked in a cake and palmed off on the unwary, it dies happy.'

Mark Twain, American author and humorist

BEYOND AWFUL BAKING JOKES #4

What do you call a chicken in a shell suit?

An egg.

CUPCAKES AROUND THE WORLD

Cupcakes are everywhere, no matter where you are or which rock you are trying to crawl under to escape them. But if you are planning on going traveling around Europe, watch out for these words – it'll be those damn, sneaky foreigners trying to sell you cupcakes.

Petits Gateaux – French
Bigné – Italian
Magdalena – Spanish

HOW TO MAKE A FLOUR BOMB

Baking is over-rated. Flour bombs aren't.

If you've got loads of leftover flour in the cupboard, make a flour bomb. Here's how …

WHAT YOU'LL NEED

A balloon
Some flour
A funnel
Paper
Masking tape

BOMBS AWAY

1. Cut out a strip of paper about ½ in (1.5cm) wide and 1⅓ in (3.5cm) long and coat one side in glue. Grab your balloon and half inflate it.
2. Hold the top of the balloon so no air escapes, and put the end of the funnel into the neck of the balloon.
3. Pour the flour inside the balloon and slowly let an equal amount of air escape at the same time. Tie up the top of the balloon.
4. Turn the balloon onto its side and pinch the balloon so you are only holding the rubber and no flour.
5. Cut a 1in (2.5cm) long hole in the side of the balloon without letting any flour escape (this step is the hardest).
6. Use your paper to cover up the hole, but hold it in place, as it will take a short period of time to stick.
7. Use the pieces of masking tape (one on each end) to stick the paper on the balloon.
8. Get it soaked, the wetter the better.
9. Now find your target ...

Alternatively, you could just throw eggs at people – much less hassle.

THERE SHALL BE NO CUPCAKES

‘It’s not the cupcake that’s the problem. The cupcake represents Americana. … It’s part of the American psyche.’

Michael Benjamin, Democrat, Bronx, N.Y.

Following a 2009 guideline report from New York’s Department of Education’s Wellness Policy and Initiatives – ‘to improve the quality and nutritional value of foods and beverages that are available for children and limit how much sugar is consumed at school’ – the Education Department banned the selling of cupcakes and sugary treats at bake sales. This caused an outcry as bake sales represented an important, and historic, moneymaking tool used by students to earn money to help finance school and extracurricular activities like pep rallies and proms.

Sounds like a good idea to me though, especially when 40 per cent of New York City’s elementary and middle school kids are overweight or obese.

$NaHCO_3 + H^+ \rightarrow Na^+ + CO_2 + H_2O$

If you want something else to blame for your cupcake addiction, apart from yourself, then blame Alfred Bird who in 1843 created what we now call baking powder. The invention of this Devil Dust (as I'm calling it) started a baking revolution around the world that, obviously, led to a rise in the consumption of fat, sugar and flour.

Baking powder is a pretty useful ingredient to have lying around the house. Here is a load of other stuff – apart from stuffing it in your mouth – that you can use it for.

1. Underarm deodorant (feel free to use a muffin as a blotter)
2. Insect bite relief
3. To relieve heartburn
4. Mouthwash
5. Fire extinguisher (seriously)
6. To draw out jellyfish venom
7. Toilet cleaner
8. To polish mirrors

CUPCAKE PORN

If you type 'cupcake porn' into any Internet browser, you'll find a pathetic 3,250,000 results staring back at you. A pretty disappointing figure, but still a huge amount of weirdos with too much time – and butter – on their hands. For context, just the word 'porn' fires back a mind-boggling 1,390,000,000 results!

QUOTECAKES #11

'I felt like a baby bunny smelling like a spring flower. I felt good ... like salt or freshly baked bread.'

Justin Bieber, Canadian pop singer

CAKETAILS

If you're going to eat a vast amount of cupcakes, and from the look of you I think you do, you might as well get completely drunk while you're at it. Here's a list of a few popular, and boozy, cupcakes sold at Caketails (American-style cupcakes that combine cupcakes and cocktails) to whet your appetite.

1. Butter Rum cupcake
2. Southern Comfort-infused cupcake
3. White Russian cupcake
4. Blue Hawaiian Tipple cupcake
5. Strawberry Champagne cupcake
6. Margarita cupcake
7. Banana Daiquiri cupcake with rum frosting
8. Peach Bellini cupcake
9. Stout cupcake with pretzel topping
10. Jack Daniel's cupcake with whiskey ganache and whiskey frosting
11. Mudslide cupcake
12. Blackberry Cabernet cupcake
13. Pina Colada cupcake
14. Whiskey Sour cupcake
15. Caramel Appletini cupcake

HOLE LOT OF DONUT

The largest donut ever made was a big ol' jelly (jam) donut. It weighed 1.7 tons (bigger than a family car) and measured 16ft (4.9m) in diameter and was 16in (41cm) high in the center.

CAKESPIRACY THEORY #5

'Cupcakes embody the postmodern ideal of the manufactured good that has been injected with artificial difference, in order to conjure a sense of individuality. Cupcakes are indie desserts. And like hipsters, cupcakes are pretty much all the same. Cupcake sprinkles and hipster scarves serve the same purpose, turning the plainly ordinary into the veiled ordinary.'

Mark Sample, 'On the Predominance of Cupcakes as a Cultural Form'

NATIONAL BAKING WEEK 2013

If you live in the UK, book your overseas holiday for the week commencing 15 October. If you live outside the UK, don't visit the week commencing 15 October.

National Baking Week starts – well what do you know! – 15 October 2013.

ALTERNATIVE TV SHOWS

Tired of watching reality baking shows on TV. Why not fantasize about watching these fictional shows instead …*

1. *Baking Bad*
2. *The Yeast Wing*
3. *The Walking Bread*
4. *30 Rock Cakes*
5. *Glee* (*Gluten-free*)
6. *CSI* (*Cream Scone Investigation*)
7. *Game of Scones*
8. *The Big Bagel Theory*
9. *The Scoffice*
10. *Two and a Half Meringues*

* I'm pretty chuffed with these.

QUOTECAKES #12

'If you wish to bake an apple pie from scratch, you must first invent the universe!'*

Carl Sagan, American astronomer and science writer

* True, but for God's sake Carl, don't forget the apples.

WE HAVE WAYS OF BAKING YOU TALK

In 2012, the home baking market in the UK soared in value by 18.2 per cent with 41 per cent of Britons claiming they now bake at least once a fortnight. An industry magazine called *The Grocer*, reported that in the years 2008–12 the home-baking market in the UK has seen profits double in size from £376 million to £645 million. Just think how buggered (and poor) we'll be in another five years …

BEAT IT, SUGAR #2

Your dentist has been telling you this stuff for years …

* In 1900, the population of the USA consumed approximately 5lb (2.3kg) of sugar per person, per year.
* In 2000, that figure had increased to about 150lb (68kg) of sugar per person, per year.
* The average American consumes 22 teaspoons of sugar every day.
* 33 per cent of the American population is obese and another 33 per cent are overweight. This means that two-thirds of the adult population is either overweight or actually obese. As I've said before, PUT DOWN THE BAKING TRAY … AND WALK AWAY.

QUOTECAKES #13

'All I do on my days off now is bake. I like to try out making different things. I have such a raging social life!'*

Taylor Swift, American singer-songwriter

* Our definition of raging seems to differ, Taylor.

KRISPYILCIOUS

The popular US company Krispy Kreme is now incredibly popular in the UK. Thanks guys! While their donuts may be super-tasty and hole-less, they are pretty unfriendly to your intestines.

So, before you take another bite, why not let your digestive tract digest these facts.

* 7.5 million donuts are made every day in the USA. The most calorific donut has 340 calories.
* 1.3 million pounds (590kg) of sprinkles are used each year.

* Each week Krispy Kreme makes enough donuts to reach from New York City to Los Angeles. That's approximately 2,790 miles (4,490km) door-to-door.

BAKER OF GOOD NEWS?

Martyn Leek, editor of *British Baker* – the awe-inspiring magazine behind National Cupcake Week, recently baked lyrical about cupcakes.

'While sales are slowing slightly, these figures show there is still growth in the cupcake market. However, bakers, cupcakers and home businesses need to work even harder on their offerings.'

Another year of cupcake misery then, folks. See you then.

FEELS LIKE WARM APPLE PIE

As the saying goes, 'There are few things as American as apple pie', but like much of America's pie tradition, the original apple pie recipe belongs to England. The Pilgrims brought their pie-making skills, along with the apple seeds, to America. As the popularity of apple pie spread throughout the nation, the phrase grew to symbolize American prosperity. You can now buy two apple pies from McDonald's for 99 cents: the pilgrims would be spinning in their graves.

NOW YOU KNOW #2

You probably shouldn't care but the average donut hole is $^{4}/_{5}$ in (2cm) in diameter.

109 MILLION CUPCAKES ON THE WALL

Grocery Analyst SymphonyIRI reported that in the UK an eye-watering 109.9 million cupcakes were sold in the 52 weeks to 11 June 2011. This figure increased marginally to 111.03 million in 2012, an increase of just 1 per cent.

ACCORDING TO GOOGLE

In 2011, cupcakes were the fastest-rising recipe search in the UK, according to Google's annual zeitgeist list.

2 BROKE GIRLS

You know that the cupcake phenomenon has grabbed popular culture by the throat when a US TV sitcom about – and I'm quoting Wikipedia here, I haven't actually watched it – 'The misadventures of two girls and their efforts to start a cupcake business in Brooklyn, New York' airs.

This comedy sitcom began in 2011–12 and has been nominated for three Emmys, winning one – for 'Art Direction' – which should tell you everything you need to know. Not that I'm one to judge …

CONCLUSION (OF SORTS); WAVE GOODBYE TO BAKING …

Forrest Gump's mom once observed that 'Life is like a box of chocolates'. And while she's not wrong metaphorically, in reality modern life – this generation – is more like a box of ludicrously-frosted cupcakes – full of crap that looks good on the surface, but is slowly killing us one moist bite at a time.

Cupcakes, baking and chowing-down on rich, fatty foods, like our current (and never-ceasing) obsession with celebrity, are bad for us. Like the influx of baking programs you see on TV all around the world, promoting baking as a wholesome pastime – an activity that takes us back to the simpler, better times before life got all crazy – the real truth is that all baked goods soften your brain and clog up your insides. And while Forrest's mum goes on to say – nay, believe – 'You never know what you're going to get' in life, the truth is, you do. It's called a heart attack.

ACKNOWLEDGMENTS

I'd like to thank Katie Hewett for her brilliant editing of my awful, atrocious and abominable over-use of alliteration. Her expert eyes are always appreciated.

I'd also like to doff my cap to all the team at Portico Books.

A Note On Sources

The American Diabetic and Dietetic Associations; www.bakersfederation.org.uk; www.bakeryinfo.co.uk; www.bbcgoodfood.com; www.cupcakefetish.com; www.dailymail.co.uk; www.express.co.uk; www.fabflour.co.uk; foodbeast.com; foodstoriesblog.com; www.foodnetwork.com; Good Housekeeping Calorie Counter; guinnessworldrecords.com; www.guardian.co.uk; www.huffingtonpost.co.uk; www.huffingtonpost.com; www.kgbanswers.com; metro.co.uk; www.mintel.com; www.mirror.co.uk; newyorkcbslocal.com; www.samplereality.com; www.simplybusiness.co.uk; sortedfood.com; topcultured.com; traceyadamson.wordpress.com; uk.lifestyle.yahoo.com; wakeup-world.com; en.wikipedia.org

First published in the United Kingdom in 2013 by
Portico Books
10 Southcombe Street
London
W14 0RA

An imprint of Anova Books Company Ltd

ISBN 9781909397194

A CIP catalogue record for this book is available from the British Library.

10 9 8 7 6 5 4 3 2 1

Printed and bound by 1010 Printing International Ltd, China

This book can be ordered direct from the publisher by
www.anovabooks.com